ears

mouths

eyes

mouths

noses

Darlyne A. Murawski

animal

faces

Sterling Publishing Co., Inc.

New York

faces

Faces can have ears,
A mouth, a nose, and eyes.
Most animals have them,
Whatever their size.

furry
face

I am a cat
with fur and whiskers
on my face. My whiskers
help me know where
I am going, especially
when it's dark.

scaly face

I am a lizard
called the bearded dragon.
My face is covered with
tough, leathery scales and
a thin skin over the top.

feathery face

I am a lovebird.

My face and body have feathers that protect my thin, sensitive skin from heat and cold.

smooth face

I am a frog.

My smooth skin helps me breathe and drink by letting air and water enter right through it.

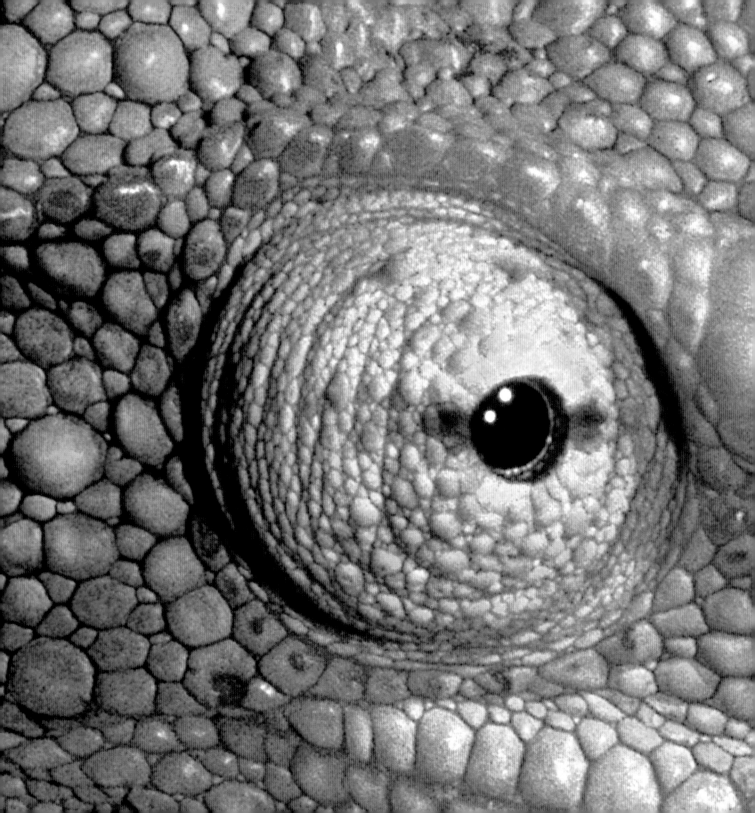

eyes

Eyes to blink,
Eyes to swivel.
Some are great big—
Others are little.

crab eyes

My eyes are on stalks.
I raise them up to look around
and fold them down when
I enter my burrow.

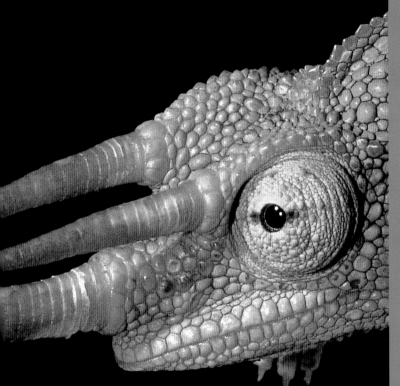

chameleon eyes

My eyes swivel in different directions.
I can look in front of me with one eye
while I look behind me with the other.

fly eyes

I have thousands of tiny eyes all packed together, so I can see above, below, and all around—all at the same time.

rooster eyes

The red in my eyes matches the red on my face, comb, and wattles. I'm the dandiest bird in the coop.

frog eyes

My big eyes see well in the dark.

I always keep an eye out for danger.

My eyes even push down in my

head to help me swallow.

cow eyes

I have a big dark eye on
each side of my head.
I can see all around me,
except for what's right
behind me.

ears

Food awaits,
Mates call,
Danger lurks.
Animals hear all!

hedgehog ears

My cupped ears help me
find my dinner. I listen
for the scurry of insects,
then I catch them and
gobble them up.

frog ears

My ears are the circles
behind my eyes. I can hear
quite well, even under water.
I listen quietly for other
frogs to call.

goat ears

My ears are long and floppy with soft and shiny little hairs. They hang down below my horns.

squirrel ears

My fuzzy little ears stand straight up. I need to be ready to run if I hear danger nearby.

They smell.
They breathe.
They sniff.
They sneeze.
They're wet.
They're dry.
Noses do as
they please.

noses

I make it my business to sniff everything. My cold, wet nose smells much better than a person's nose.

dog nose

lizard nose

My nose has two tiny holes in front of my eyes. But don't let the size fool you. I have a keen sense of smell.

elephant
nose

My trunk is much more than just a nose. It puts food in my mouth, picks things up, and can even give me a shower.

My soft, furry nose helps me find my favorite food—grasses. It also alerts me to danger.

sheep
nose

mouths

Chew, bite,

Snip, lick,

Drink, slice,

Grind, click,

Bark, chirp,

Howl, hiss,

Mouths are able

to do all of this!

turtle
mouth

My mouth has no teeth, but its sharp edges slice my food when I bite. I hiss when I feel threatened.

My mouth has black jaws to cut and grind up leaves. My yellow upper lip and brown lower lip hold in the food when I chew.

katydid
mouth

Don't be fooled by my
toothy grin. I have
sharp teeth and
powerful jaws that
snap shut when
I hunt down a meal.

alligator mouth

snake mouth

I can open my mouth so wide that I can eat animals bigger than my own head.

My mouth is in the middle of my body. I use my little tube feet to feed myself.

starfish mouth

sloth mouth

I have a messy little mouth from eating leaves up in a treetop in the rain forest. I eat and move very slowly.

butterfly mouth

My mouth is like a straw. When I'm finished drinking, I roll it up close to my head.

eyes

mouths

noses

Library of Congress Cataloging-in-Publication Data Available

2 4 6 8 10 9 7 5 3 1

Published by Sterling Publishing Co., Inc.
387 Park Avenue South, New York, NY 10016
Copyright © 2005 by Darlyne A. Murawski
Distributed in Canada by Sterling Publishing
c/o Canadian Manda Group, 165 Dufferin Street
Toronto, Ontario, Canada M6K 3H6
Distributed in Great Britain and Europe by Chris Lloyd at Orca Book
Services, Stanley House, Fleets Lane, Poole BH15 3AJ, England
Distributed in Australia by Capricorn Link (Australia) Pty. Ltd.
P.O. Box 704, Windsor, NSW 2756, Australia

Printed in China

Sterling ISBN 1-4027-2295-8